Captain John Casinov has two loves in his life—his family and his work. When his son, Jonathan, and the man's family visits from Santa Cruz—primarily to try to convince him to retire and move south—John takes advantage of one of his detective's offer. He accepts a bunch of free passes to the marine park, World of Aquatica. While there, he finds his interest snagged by a big, friendly, black-haired man. The handsome man brazenly introduces himself as William Roush . . . then he asks John on a date. While he's flattered, John laughs it off while declining. Undeterred, William approaches John a second time later that day, so he accepts. Imagine his surprise when John discovers who William actually is—the partial owner of the marine park. John doesn't understand why a man who's young, confident, and rich—who could have anyone he wants—would pursue him. When William shares that shifters are real, John wonders at the man's sanity . . . until William actually proves it. Can John come to grips with his newfound knowledge and accept William into his life? Or will retiring and running be the decision of the day?

Drifting With a Giant Squid
Copyright © 2019 Charlie Richards
ISBN: 978-1-4874-2475-6
Cover art by Angela Waters

Published by eXtasy Books Inc or
Devine Destinies, an imprint of eXtasy Books Inc

Look for us online at:
www.eXtasybooks.com or www.devinedestinies.com

Drifting With a Giant Squid Beneath Aquatica's Waves Book 5

By

Charlie Richards

DEDICATION

The truth is a snare. You cannot have it without being caught. You cannot have the truth in such a way that you catch it, but only in such a way that it catches you.

CHAPTER ONE

"Dad, have you thought about what we talked about the other night at all?"

Damn. Being trapped in my son's SUV, riding shotgun, means I'm a fucking captive audience.

In truth, Captain John Casinov had avoided thinking about Jonathan's encouragement of retiring—plus his offer to help him move south. John loved his job. True, he loved Jonathan and his son's family, too, but he was way too young to retire.

God, I'm only . . . huh . . . fifty-one, already.

In this day and age, that's still really young, though.

John had worked damn hard to earn his captain's position. While on occasion he found the rote administration duties tedious, he still enjoyed the few cases he took on as well as the camaraderie of his boys in blue. The guys on the force were a second family.

"Dad?"

Lying through his teeth—and swallowing back a huff of annoyance by humming—John told him, "Yeah, I thought about it. You know I like visiting you all, Jon." He focused on his son and forced a reassuring smile. "But I can't imagine what I would do down there." Reaching over the space between the comfortable chairs, he squeezed Jonathan's bicep in a show of fatherly appreciation. "Give me a few more years, huh, son? I really like where I'm at."

Jonathan's eyebrows furrowed as he glanced John's way. He opened his mouth, and John spotted it a mile away. His son was going to launch into another spiel about why it was a good idea for him to move.

Just as quickly, Jonathan's features shifted into a wide smile. His hazel eyes—so similar to John's own—twinkled. "Well, I have a couple lady friends down there that are really looking forward to meeting you." Jonathan winked as he told him, "They're both in their forties, I think." Scoffing, his son added, "You know it's not polite to ask a lady about such things, but they sure gush over your pictures on the mantel whenever they come over for dinner."

Huh. Okay. That's not the direction I thought Jon would take this.

Unwilling to discuss his love life with his son—or lack thereof, actually—John focused on another aspect of Jonathan's words. "I'm kinda curious why you have ladies in their forties over at your house."

"Oh. Ha." Jonathan rolled his eyes before glancing in the rearview mirror. "They're part of Grace's Bible study group. Hey, Grace. Tell my dad about Molly and Linda."

John turned in his seat to regard his daughter-in-law. He knew Grace was very active in the church their family attended in Santa Cruz. Not only did Grace lead a women's Bible study, but she also taught the eight-to-ten-year-old class of children's church every Sunday morning.

While John wasn't particularly religious, when he visited them, he would attend services, too. John adopted an approach more geared toward *to each his own as long as you don't try to shove it down anyone else's throat.* Over his many years on the force, John had seen many cases where religious organizations had done fantastic things for a community. Unfortunately, he'd also found many cases where religious zealots could be dangerous to the community, too.

When Grace lifted her focus from her *Women's World* magazine, the athletic blonde smiled at them. "I'm sorry, honey. What was that?"

Jonathan repeated himself, an indulgent smile curving his lips.

"Oh!" Grace's smile widened, and her blue eyes twinkled. She even laughed softly before saying, "Molly and Linda are in my Bible study, and both are lovely women." Leaning forward, Grace touched John's upper arm. "Both inside and out. And boy do they sure ask about you, Father. They would both love to meet you." Grinning, she added, "I know we've never really talked about what interests you in a lady or if you're even interested in dating, but is there something I can tell you about them that might interest you in coming down for a date?"

It always warmed John's heart when Grace called him Father. He loved the kind-hearted and beautiful woman Jonathan had managed to win the affections of. With John working so many hours, Jonathan had spent much of his time first at daycare, then at school, youth centers, and even after school sports activities. John sometimes didn't even feel as if he'd raised his son.

The years have flown by so very swiftly. And now my grandkids are fifteen and twelve. Just wow! Hmm . . . maybe this is something I need to think a bit more about.

John cleared his throat as he took in Grace's expectant expression. Feeling his cheeks heat a little, he opened his mouth, then closed it again. Glancing at Jonathan, John saw his son's ever-so-slight smirk.

It hit him suddenly that he'd totally been set up.

How long has Grace been urging Jon to make some kind of comment like this?

"Well." John drew the word out slowly, thinking quickly. "I admit it's been a while since I've thought about dating."

As in, almost seventeen years when Jonathan was dating Grace.

"I have pictures on my phone," Grace stated suddenly. Leaning down, she grabbed her purse. "Let me show you."

As she began shoving her magazine into her purse, obviously preparing to pull out her phone, Jonathan countered, "How about we do that at lunch, dear? We're here."

Never had John been so happy to arrive at his destination. It wasn't that he didn't feel flattered to hear that he sparked the interest of some random women. John just wasn't certain he wanted to deal with figuring out how to please a woman again. He'd failed epically the first time, after all.

But I've never shared I would be more interested in dating a guy, either.

Fighting back a sigh, John dismissed the whole issue. It didn't matter anyway. He'd never met a man who'd interested him enough to make him want to crack that door.

"Wow, kids! Look at this place," Grace called, pointing out the window to the right. "It's huge! Father, how did you hear about it? Is it new?"

Appreciating the subject change, John stated, "It's been here over ten years, now, I think. So fairly new." He pointed toward the entrance indicating VIP parking before grabbing a mirror hanger from his wallet and hanging it. "One of my detectives, uh, Detective Grisham Canton, he hooked up with a guy who works here about six months ago and moved in with him." Laughing, John added, "Never thought of Grisham as the settling down type, but he's head-over-heels for Cuzco. A very cute couple. They're the ones who gave me these free passes and the VIP parking tag."

John watched as Jonathan's brows shot up. "An openly gay couple in homicide?" he commented as he stopped at the booth and rolled down the window. "That's new." Then he turned and greeted the person manning the booth and took the map he offered, saying, "Thank you." Jonathan listened as the man told him where to park.

Once Jonathan had started the SUV moving again, John revealed, "Actually, not so much. There are a number of men—and even a couple of women—who are open about their sexuality." John found himself fascinated to hear his family's response . . . and his heart even pounded a little harder in his chest. "Discrimination is dealt with harshly . . . *any* kind of discrimination."

"Huh." Jonathan's brows furrowed, but he didn't say anything else as he guided the SUV through the lot.

"Well, that's lovely." Grace's response drew John's attention to his daughter-in-law, and he took in her smiling countenance as she was gathering the bags and urging their children to get ready to exit the vehicle. "I hope we have a chance to thank them sometime. It's awfully nice that they would get passes for us all." Pointing at Anita, their fifteen-year-old daughter, she stated, "Hand me that sunscreen, would you, sweetie?"

Anita pulled her attention from her phone and grabbed the tube of sunscreen she'd left on the seat beside her. While handing it to her mother, she commented, "Carley is a lesbian, Dad. Didn't you know?" Then she turned back to Grace. "I pulled up the map of this place on my phone. Can we go to the left, first? There's a pool where you can pet stingrays." The teenager's blue eyes gleamed with excitement. "And I read that our passes are the special ones that include tickets to a tiger shark show. How cool is that? There's a showing in about an hour and a half at ten-thirty. Can we see it?"

"A tiger shark?" their twelve-year-old son, Pryce, piped up. "Awesome! Can we go?"

"Oh, that does sound exciting," Grace replied as she pushed open her door. "Hon, don't let me forget to order a gift basket as a thank you for Dad's nice detective and his partner."

Having parked the SUV and turning it off a moment before, Jonathan cleared his throat. Even though his cheeks were just a slight bit pink, he replied, "Of course, Grace."

John smiled to himself as he followed his family toward

the entrance of *World of Aquatica.*

Damn, how did my son end up with such a good woman?

Still, John couldn't help but wonder if Grace would be that welcoming if the notion of dating a man came from her father-in-law.

William Roush grinned broadly as he glanced around at the over a dozen kids and parents clustered around the stingray pool. The walls of the cement pond were two feet high, but the interior was only a foot deep. The bottom was coated with sand, and inside the pool swam four stingrays.

Two were real stingrays, and two were shifters.

As a shifter himself, William could easily see the differences. Unknowing humans, however, would only recognize that two were larger than the other pair. The bigger ones were making it easy for the youngsters crowding around the pool to reach in and brush their fingers over their upper backs.

"Now these guys might not look aggressive," William warned as he monitored those around the pool's actions. "But they *are* related to sharks." Seeing several kids' heads pop up, their eyes focusing more fully on him, William settled into a serious expression. "Stingrays use their tails not only for maneuvering, but also for defense . . . and that can be dangerous, since they have venomous and spined tails." Snapping his fingers to draw the attention of a teenager who was petting a little too close to the back of one of the shifter's bodies, William cautioned, "That's why you're only to pet these guys on their upper back near their head."

Once the wide-eyed boy nodded and returned to stroking Gillian where he should, William swept his gaze over the others in the area. He knew the female stingray shifter would never harm a human while she was on duty in the petting pool, but that didn't mean one of the non-shifters wouldn't. William's job at the pool — as well as Serena's, who he was teamed up with that day — was not only to assure the health of the stingrays but to keep the humans safe, too.

"Isn't it a stingray that killed that famous animal expert guy?" William turned his attention to the right, so he could focus on the speaker — an athletic-looking teenage girl with blonde hair and blue eyes. She cocked her head and narrowed her eyes, then burst out, "Steve Irwin, right?"

William nodded, all the while betting her parents were just dreading the moment the pretty girl started dating. "That's right." Wincing, he shook his head. "He was filming an underwater documentary and was pierced in the heart by a stingray barb." Sweeping his gaze around the area, William cautioned, "That goes to show that even someone experienced with animals *can* have an accident. No matter the animal, *always* be careful."

Many of the children bobbed their heads in acknowledgment. Some of the adults did, too.

"You really let just anyone pet something so dangerous?"

Turning back to his right again, William looked beyond the teenager to a dark-haired man who was most likely her father — judging by the way he pulled her hand away from the pool. "Think of it as taking your kids to the county swimming pool," William told him, smiling as he ignored the guy's abrasive tone. "There are rules put in place for everyone's safety as well as a lifeguard on duty." William pointed at a sign on the far wall. "No climbing into the pool. No touching a stingray's tail. Always listen to the instructor. Be gentle." Offering a disarming smile, he continued, "Our stingrays are used to being touched, but we work very hard to keep everyone safe. In *World of Aquatica's* eleven-year history, we've never had a single sting."

William knew that was in part due to the fact that the shifter stingrays easily kept the others calm. Hell, if there'd been a giant squid petting aquarium, William would have happily allowed the humans to touch him. That kind of exhibit would have been damn impossible to explain, however, no matter how much money it would bring in.

He and his older brother, Kaiser — their pod's alpha — had even discussed it once.

His words must have placated the man — either that or it was the way his wife rested her hand on his arm and stated, "Relax, Jonathan. This is why we came over here," for the guy nodded and backed off.

Once the human had moved backward, allowing his two children access to the pool, William found his attention snagged by a third adult. This one was obviously older with gray at his temples and short, salt and pepper hair. He wore jeans that showed off muscular legs and a light jacket that did nothing to hide his wide shoulders and trim form.

While William pegged the human as being in his late forties or early fifties, he thought he still looked amazing. His mouth watered with a desire to taste his full lips which were curved into a smile as he peered into the pool and guided the younger sibling's hand so he could pet Carlton, the second shifter in the pool. Even his blood heated and flowed south, causing his prick to plump.

Curious at his body's reactions — and feeling his squid urge him forward — William drifted closer to the man. That was when he smelled the subtle, slightly salty aroma mixed with a masculine scent. Inhaling deeply even as William glanced around — he still had a job to do, after all — he analyzed the scent more fully.

Oh, fuck a duck!

Excited realization coursed through William.

This human is my mate!

William couldn't stop the huge grin that curved his lips. A shiver of anticipation rolled through him as he swept his gaze over the man again. He licked his lips, then swallowed hard as he swiftly thought about ideas on how to woo the human.

The first step is obvious.

Seeing the way the young man was having trouble reaching Carlton, William took it as his opening to get closer to the pair ... and his mate. "Hey, buddy," he greeted the youngster. "Let me help." William reached out and, using his much longer reach, touched Carlton's side and guided him closer to the pool's edge. Grinning at the boy, William added, "Don't try that at home, buddy. These guys know me."

"Thanks!" the youngster immediately replied, turning his attention to the stingray. "And I won't!"

William straightened. After a quick glance around, he turned his attention to the older human. He held out his hand and offered him a winning smile. "Hi, I'm William Roush. And you are?"

The older human's brows lifted high on his forehead, but he took his hand. "John Casinov."

The name jogged William's memory. "Oh, you're the captain at Detective Canton's precinct. Good to meet you." *Very, very good to meet you.* "He speaks well of you."

The two times Grisham mentioned the captain, it had been in a good light, after all.

"That's nice to know," John replied, tugging his hand, since William hadn't bothered to release him.

"I've always found your job fascinating," William told him, finally letting go of his mate's hand. That might have been a stretch—a big one—but William sure felt that way now. "Will you have dinner with me tomorrow? I'd love to hear all about it."

John's lips parted in an inviting way, betraying his shock. His cheeks took on a pinkish hue, and he glanced around swiftly. He even swallowed so hard his Adam's apple bobbed.

William waited impatiently, peering down at the slightly shorter man and holding his gaze.

"Oh, you're serious?" John laughed as he shifted his weight from foot to foot. He even swept his gaze down, then back up, William's body. For an instant, it seemed he might accept. Then John glanced beyond William before meeting his gaze. "I'm flattered. Really. But I have my son and his family in town, so I'm not available." With a smile that appeared to hold a hint of disappointment—same as the scent that John was giving off—the captain stated, "My family's moving on. Thanks for your help getting the stingray over here for Pryce to pet. That was really kind of you."

Then John brushed past William.

William turned and watched him go, pleased when he saw how John peered over his shoulder at him. Narrowing his eyes, William gave the man a once-over, allowing the human to see the desire he felt for him. John's cheeks pinked once more, and he turned away.

"Oh, my mate," William muttered to himself. "You won't get away that easily."

"Everything okay?" Serena asked, touching William's arm and drawing his attention. The dolphin shifter's gaze held concern.

William nodded. "I'm pretty fantastic." He grinned at Serena. "That man is my mate."

Letting out a little squeak, Serena hugged him, then bounced back a step. "Congratulations, Beta William!"

"Thanks. I'm gonna step away for just a sec," William told her. "I need to call my brother." He didn't mention that he was going to call Eban, their head enforcer, so he could have his mate discreetly followed.

"Of course."

William crossed to a quiet corner as he pulled out his phone. As he waited for Kaiser to pick up, he realized it was a damn good thing they always had two people on duty when they had stingrays in the pool, because William knew he would be very distracted for the two-plus hours remaining on his shift.

CHAPTER TWO

Even as John sank the tines of his fork into his fillet of grilled, wild-caught salmon, his mind drifted back to the big, good-looking man at the stingray petting pool. *William.* His wide, friendly smile in his handsome face had caused John's heart to trip wildly in his chest. The way his deep green eyes had heated as he'd watched John walk away—

Just thinking about it caused John's blood to fire in his veins. Even his groin warmed, and his prick plumped.

John couldn't remember the last time his body had responded just from a look. It had definitely been over a decade. Some of that was probably due to the fact that after his son had married and moved, he'd buried himself in work.

Empty nest syndrome, some had said.

Any way John looked at it, he'd sure liked the way William's attraction had made him respond. The big guy had been damn hot, too. Unfortunately, being asked out by a man in front of his family—who'd already been heading away from the pool—John just hadn't been able to get himself to respond.

It was too big a step . . . especially while out in public.

John wondered if he would ever meet the man again.

Dismissing the notion in favor of listening to his grandkids chatter excitedly about the different exhibits they'd checked out as well as the tiger shark show they'd just come from, John couldn't help but smile. He loved that something he'd planned had given them such joy. It didn't surprise John that Pryce had thought the shark eating raw, dripping

12

chunks of meat was *way cool* — his words. Fortunately, Anita had enjoyed it, too, calling the shark magnificent.

At a lull in the conversation, Pryce stated, "That guy where we were petting stingrays asked Grampa on a date."

The side conversation between Jonathan and Grace where they were pouring over the map ceased. Both of their heads popped up. Grace's brows were lifted a bit on her forehead, and Jonathan's lips were parted in obvious surprise . . . but something more.

Scandalized, maybe.

John forced a rough chuckle from his too-dry throat. "William didn't say *date*, Pryce," he countered, reaching over to ruffle his hair.

Predictably, the twelve-year-old pulled away while rolling his eyes.

"What *did* he say?" Grace asked curiously as she used her fork to stab a large fry.

"He knows Grisham and recognized my name as the captain of my precinct," John told them, doing his best to downplay the interaction. "He said he was interested in getting together and talking about what it's like."

"That's a date," Anita piped up, grinning at him. She lifted her hand toward him in a fist. "Rock on, Gramps. He was good lookin' for an older guy."

Unable to help himself, John laughed softly. He didn't leave his granddaughter hanging. Lifting his own fist, he bumped it against hers.

At the same time, John commented, "So, if he's an old guy, what does that make me?" He wasn't sure if he wanted to hear the answer.

Anita grinned brightly at him. "You're Gramps. You don't have an age."

John swallowed around the lump in his throat while nodding. "Thanks." Scooping up another forkful of fish and rice, he shoved it into his mouth.

For a second, John thought that would be the end of it.

Then Jonathan commented with disdain in his tone, "So did you tell him to take a hike?"

"No," John replied, drawing out the word. "I—"

"Holy shit," Jonathan hissed, leaning across the table in the curved booth they were seated in. His cheeks had taken on a ruddy color. "You're going on a date with a guy?" Jonathan scowled even as he shook his head in obvious disbelief. "Is that why you haven't dated? Why you hardly gave Molly and Linda's pictures a second look? Are you a—"

"Honey, language," Grace cut in, scowling sternly from her position next to him.

John could guess at what his son had intended to say, and the word probably wouldn't be a kind one considering his tone.

"I think a little cussing is understandable when Dad's dropping a bombshell like this," Jonathan countered, waving his fork in John's direction. Good thing it was empty.

"I haven't dropped any bombshells," John stated, hoping to diffuse the situation. He didn't want to see Jonathan and his wife fight. "I told William that I was flattered but unavailable. Then I hurried and caught up with you all."

Jonathan didn't seem to want to give an inch. Resting his forearm on the table, he pressed, "So if we *weren't* in town and you *were* available, you'da said yes?"

"Please, calm down, Jon," John murmured even as frustration slithered through him. He bit back his desire to sigh. Holding his son's gaze, John saw a mutinous gleam in Jonathan's eyes—one that he hadn't seen in over a decade. Realizing no matter what he said was going to cause his son to get bent out of shape, John figured it might as well be for the truth. "His offer for dinner was tempting. After all, like Anita said"—he waved absently toward his granddaughter, who was sitting directly to his right—"William is a good-looking guy. Even if it was just as a friend, I don't have many of them outside the department, so that would be good, too." Then John shrugged and curved his lips into a small smile. "If it progressed into something more? Well, like you said. It's been a while. Having someone in my life would be a good thing, right?"

Seeing the way Jonathan's mouth hung open made John realize his son hadn't expected him to admit anything head-on. He also saw the gleam of revulsion in his eyes, and as his son closed his mouth, it twisted into disgust. His cheeks continued to darken.

John knew an explosion was imminent.

Fortunately, Grace recovered first. "That man seemed very nice and knowledgeable. Pryce told me how he helped him." While she smiled, there was a worried tightness around her eyes—probably put there because she kept cutting side-eyed glances at Jon. "Maybe after we leave you could come and see him again. Ask *him* out. Hmm?"

"You're okay with the idea of Dad going on a d-d-d—" Evidently, Jonathan couldn't even get the word out.

Not wanting to have something like this hashed out in the restaurant, John decided to give his son a few minutes to collect himself. "I'm gonna slip off to the men's room," he stated, placing his napkin beside his half-eaten plate. John smiled at everyone as he rose. "I'll be back in a minute."

John headed toward the sign indicating the restrooms. Turning into the hallway, he paused, surprise rippling through him. There, leaning against the wall across from the men's room door, stood William.

His heartrate spiking for a whole different reason, John swept his gaze over the male. With his hands shoved in his cargo shorts' pockets and his legs crossed at the ankles, William screamed confidence. John found it damn sexy.

William grinned at John as he pushed off the wall and

took the two steps needed to close the distance between them. "I heard what you said, John." His voice sounded like a deep, smooth rumble. "Does that mean you'll accept my offer for a date after all?" His deep green eyes glimmered with a hungry light. "And make no mistake, John. It *is* a date."

Figuring he was already causing upheaval in his life, John decided he might as well go all the way. "Yeah." Butterflies bumped in his belly, and his groin tingled at the triumphant smile that spread across William's face.

"Give me your phone, John," William ordered, holding out his hand. "I'm gonna put my number in it, and after the chaos with your son settles this evening, you're gonna call me."

John obeyed, not even questioning how William knew about his family issues.

"So, how is it going with your mate?"

William slouched in his recliner and scowled at his brother.

"That good, huh?"

Kaiser narrowed his eyes as he swept an assessing gaze over him. He tapped his forefinger on his tumbler of amber liquid—scotch that he'd brought over to share with William. His brother, older by eight years, always seemed to know when he was struggling.

William and Kaiser were close. Always had been. While most squid shifters were solitary—like their animal counterparts—Kaiser had stuck beside William. Maybe it was because they hadn't turned out to be the same species of squid. William had taken after their mother, while Kaiser their father.

Maybe sire would be a better word. The male certainly hadn't been around much.

16

"William?"

Kaiser's stern tone redrew William's attention.

William couldn't help but smile at that. That was another difference between them. While William was thought of as the happy-go-lucky and fun-loving brother, Kaiser was known for his seriousness and intensity. William figured that was because at the age of sixteen — when William was only eight — fishermen had killed their mother while she was in her animal form. They'd never seen their father again, so Kaiser had raised William.

Over the almost three centuries of their long lives, their relationship had easily morphed from parent and son to their natural brotherhood. Every once in a while, though, Kaiser reverted to the worried father. Normally William teased him when it happened.

Not this time.

"We talk on the phone every evening," William told Kaiser as he eased his recliner back, kicking his feet up. He was careful not to spill his own tumbler of scotch. "The calls are always short, because his son, Jonathan, and his family are staying with him, so he's not getting a whole lot of alone time at the moment."

Furrowing his brows, William frowned into his drink, swirling the liquid and watching the light play across the amber fluid. "I know he's feeling a little guilty, too, because while his son is not very accepting, the wife is. Even Anita is annoyed with Jonathan because her best friend at home, Carley, is a lesbian." Shaking his head, William added, "Then there's Pryce, who's just confused and feeling a little guilty. I guess he's the one who shared with the family that I asked John on a date, so he thinks the tension is his fault."

After pouring all that out, William took a sip of his scotch. "We talked a lot about family, but little else." He scoffed before adding, "Not like I can share much about myself with him, yet."

"So, you're feeling guilty because you want John, but you hate that your presence is causing your mate problems," Kaiser stated astutely. As William responded by nodding, Kaiser hummed thoughtfully. He tipped his head to the side before saying quietly, "William, you're not responsible for John's son's bigoted attitude. That's all on Jonathan."

William sighed, running his free hand through his shoulder-length black hair and scratching at his scalp. "I know." He pulled his hair band out in the process. Giving his brother a wry smile, William admitted, "It's been four days since I met the man, and I'm getting a bit anxious. So's my animal. I want him. See him. Touch him. Feel what his lips and body feel like against mine. I—"

Groaning, William shoved back to a sitting position before downing the rest of his scotch. He rubbed the bridge of his nose. Just thinking about doing those things had his prick hard and aching behind the fly of his shorts.

Kaiser chuckled, the sound rusty and low.

William snapped his attention to his brother. He knew what that kind of dark laugh meant. The other shifter had an idea pinging through his brain.

Will I like it?

Laughing louder, Kaiser grinned broadly. "Don't give me that look."

The relaxed expression on his serious brother had the same effect on William. His heart rate slowed. Lifting one brow, William gave Kaiser his *what look* expression.

Kaiser rose and snatched William's tumbler from his fingers. "What I mean is," he began as he headed to the sideboard where he'd left the liquor. Half-turning as he refilled their glasses, Kaiser kept part of his attention on William. "You've given the mate-pull four days to build. It does affect the human, too, remember?"

After William nodded, Kaiser twisted the cap back on the scotch bottle and picked up both tumblers. "It's time we get you some help," he stated, holding out one glass. William took it automatically, and Kaiser continued, "Is John still working while his family is in town? Or is he on vacation, too?"

"John took the first week off, but he goes back to work on Monday," William told Kaiser. Before taking a sip, he added, "His son and family are staying a second week, then leaving Friday evening."

"Good," Kaiser responded, drawing out the word as he returned to his chair. Resting his forearms on his thighs, he cradled the tumbler between his palms. Kaiser pinned his intense focus on him, his lips curving into a reassuring smile. "At the moment, the rumor that you found your mate in a guy named John has made the rounds, but few know specifics about the man. It's time to change that."

William took a sip of his scotch before nodding slowly. "What did you have in mind?" Cocking his head, he added, "I don't want John made anxious because others begin *accidently* bumping into him"—he used his free hand to make air quotes—"and saying things that make him uncomfortable."

"Not what I meant," Kaiser assured. "What I do mean is that it's time we bring in Grisham. He'll understand the mate-pull, since he's mated with Cuzco. Plus, he already knows the captain." Grinning, Kaiser added, "If you haven't talked about food, yet, he can help you come up with something to take him for lunch at work." Kaiser grinned and waggled his brows. "From what I hear, due to John's influence, Grisham's precinct is very accepting of homosexual relationships." Then he turned serious. "And if you don't want to out him, you can always go as a representative of *World of Aquatica*, and you're following up on Solomon's case."

Warming to Kaiser's idea, William nodded slowly. Excitement surged through him, and even his squid vocalized in his mind. His breathing sped up.

One way or another, soon, I will see my mate.

CHAPTER THREE

John knew he should feel guilty about being happy that he'd returned to work that morning. Unfortunately, things were so tense at his house that he couldn't drum up the emotion. Whenever Grace wasn't around, Jonathan would pester John about what he'd admitted, asking him what was wrong with him and was it something his mother had done to make him think about trying out the other side of the fence.

It was the snide comment of, "You actually *like* your prostate exams?" that had really pissed John off. Only years of exerting self-control with perps had kept him from telling his son to shut the fuck up. John had figured Jonathan wouldn't understand, but he hadn't anticipated the animosity it generated in him. Grace had even apologized more than once for his behavior.

When Grace had walked into the living room and overheard Jonathan grumble, "I'd rather have you stay single than be a cocksucker," her face had turned beet red. She'd glanced around swiftly, probably making certain that the kids weren't around to hear.

John had replied, "It is *your* decision to feel that way," then excused himself. He'd heard them begin arguing in hushed tones even before he'd made it down the hall to his bedroom.

Later, Grace had cornered him and whispered, "I'm so sorry Jonathan is saying these things. I honestly don't know where they're coming from." She'd sighed heavily before telling him, "He's worked with a couple gay men at his job for years. He's never talked about them snidely. This doesn't make sense."

Sighing, John rested his hand on Grace's shoulder and squeezed reassuringly. "Accepting it in an abstract manner, like working with someone, is very different than having a family member in a same-sex relationship." John smiled warmly and added, "I'm grateful for your support, Grace. Something like this, it's probably messing with his own identity since he's always thought of me as this rugged, straight cop. I'm sure he just needs some time to accept that his father could find another man interesting in a romantic sense."

Grace had nodded as she'd nibbled her bottom lip. Then she'd leaned close and whispered, "I think Carley might be a bit more than a friend to Anita, if you know what I mean." Even as John had nodded, catching her hint that perhaps their daughter swung both ways, too, Grace continued, "So if Jon is acting like this with you, I fear how—" She paused and wrung her hands, glancing around furtively.

John understood Grace's concern. If Jonathan couldn't handle his father being in a gay relationship, how would he react to discovering his daughter may want to be in one, too? Would he be as big an ass to Anita as he was to him?

"You and the kids will always have my support," John had encouraged. "We'll get through this."

Back behind his desk, processing paperwork and reading updates on his detectives' cases, John began to relax for the first time in five days. He felt glad that this issue was coming out with him instead of Anita, but he needed a little time away from the toxic atmosphere. Plus, here at work, John knew he'd have the support of those he worked with.

Six months before, when Grisham had begun a perma-nent relationship with Cuzco, John had made certain everyone in the department knew bigoted behavior and discrimination would not be tolerated. It had caused one detective to go off the rails, and he'd attempted to murder Grisham. The man had been dirty anyway, had been in the process of being investigated by Internal Affairs, and he'd eventually been sent to prison for more than just that.

Speaking of Grisham.

Hearing the detective's voice through his partially open door, John was tempted to go talk to him. He had the odd urge to ask Grisham if he'd seen William recently, and if so, had he said anything about him. Then he realized how high school-ish that sounded.

God, a few phone calls and I'm obsessing.

John would never admit to anyone just how much he looked forward to those damn phone calls he shared with William every evening. There was just something about the way that William always seemed so happy to hear from him that caused his heart to swell. On top of that, other things swelled just listening to William's deep voice rumble in his ear, too.

In fact, just thinking about it caused his blood to heat and flow south.

Rolling his eyes in response to his thoughts, John rose to his feet. He needed to focus on work or—

"You sure the captain won't mind me barging in on him? I'm hoping for an update."

The sound of William's voice caused John's feet to freeze—his body, however, not so much. Heat rushed through his veins. Surely he had imagined—

"Come on back, William," Grisham replied. Then with a laugh, he added, "I'll see if he has a minute. Although, with the way that food from *Mishka's* smells, I don't see how he would say no, and if he does, I get first dibs."

William's warm chuckles washed over John's senses, and goose bumps broke out on his arms. A shiver of awareness slithered through him as his blood flowed south. On top of that, he felt an odd wash of emotions that it took a couple of heartbeats to identity.

There was excitement and anticipation, sure, but underneath that, there was a bit of the little green monster — jealousy. John didn't like the fact that someone else had made William laugh. It made no sense, especially since John didn't have any hold on the man.

"Come on."

"Thanks, Grish."

Upon hearing the pair's exchange, John swiftly sat back down behind his desk. He stared at his computer monitor and tapped on his keyboard, pretending to work on . . . anything. No way did he want the other men to realize he was listening and waiting for his first sight of William in six days with bated breath.

When Grisham knocked on the door and stuck his head in, asking if he had a minute, John barely had enough blood in his brain cells to answer in the affirmative and invite him in. All he could focus on was the handsome man standing behind the detective. His memory of William didn't do him justice.

As John admired William's wavy black hair, which was pulled back away from his face, along with his warm green eyes and wide smile, all he could think was — *why the hell is he bothering with me?*

"Thank you for seeing me," William stated, doing his best to sound formal . . . just in case someone outside the office was listening. He saw the slightly shell-shocked expression on John's face, and it filled him with pride that he'd put it there. William appreciated the scent of arousal lightly perfuming the air, too.

My mate definitely feels the pull. Hell yeah.

Before John had a chance to speak, Grisham closed the captain's office door. The detective had assured William that as long as the blinds were drawn and they didn't get too loud, no one would be any the wiser regarding what happened between them. While William could think of all the fantastic ways he could take advantage of that, he knew better than to try the first time he was there.

Striding forward slowly, William smiled at John. "I hope you don't mind. I got tired of waiting." Shrugging unrepentantly, he added, "I'm not always a patient man." William set the bag containing their lunch on John's desk. "I did make it seem as if I was here for a case update, so no one would think twice about me being ensconced in here with you." As William spoke, he crossed to the window and used the plastic stick to close the shade's slats. All the rest were already done.

John finally seemed to find his tongue. "Sooo, I'm guessing Grisham is in on getting you in here to see me." Rubbing the back of his neck, he flicked his gaze toward the closed door before refocusing on William. His brows furrowed as he cocked his head. "And why would those men you just walked past think I would make time for you?" His cheeks pinked as he smirked. "No offense."

William cleared his throat as he rested his knuckles on John's desk and leaned toward him. "Well, I wasn't gonna tell you this until we'd had a date or two." Seeing the way John's brows ratcheted up and how his shoulders tensed as he straightened in his seat, William lifted a hand in placation. "Nothing bad. Just didn't want to scare ya off." Curving his lips into a wry smile, he told him, "My brother is Kaiser, and I . . . well, *we* own the majority shares of *World of Aquatica*." Pointing his thumb over his shoulder, William told John, "Your people out there think I'm here to follow up on the open case of Solomon Lynch's abduction and attempted murder."

John's jaw sagged open as he stared at him with wide eyes. "Shit, I was so tempted to look you up, but since Jonathan was in town, I never took the time." Shaking his head, he waved toward the bag of *take out* food. "So? What did you bring? We can eat, and you can tell me why you've decided to pursue an older guy like me. Is it a game? Sport? For entertainment?"

William had been afraid John would respond with something like that. "Could it possibly be something as simple as . . . I find you attractive?" Glancing between the wrapped food he pulled from the plastic sack and John's face, he continued, "Grish said your favorite sub from *Mishka's Subs & Wraps* is a hot wing sub with blue cheese dressing and extra hot sauce."

Placing the referred to item halfway across the desk in front of John, William winked as he added, "Don't worry. I brought plenty of napkins." Those he added to the desk, too. "Now, myself, I prefer their lobster and crab salad in pita bread. I always get plenty, so if you want to try a bite, I wouldn't mind."

Once William had everything set before them, he used the toes of his right foot to hook the leg of one of the chairs. He pulled it close, then settled on it. Grabbing one of the wrapped pitas, William began to open it.

A wealth of pleasure surged through William when he saw John finally reach for his food. His animal liked providing a meal for his mate—even if they had purchased it from a restaurant. The urge to care for John was damn hard to resist, and William appreciated that he could finally start to give in to it.

"So, then . . ." John began slowly as he unwrapped his sub. Licking his lips, he hummed as he stared at his food. "These are so damn good but the calories." Even as he picked up half, John shook his head and sighed. "I'm gonna have to spend an extra thirty minutes in the gym for the next week because of this."

Then John took a big bite, moaning softly around his mouthful of warm food.

William grinned as he picked up his large pita pocket full of seafood salad. His animal vocalized hungrily in his mind as his stomach growled. He knew he should've eaten breakfast, but he'd been too excited. His stomach had been full of butterflies anyway.

Since William didn't want to appear as a glutton in front of his mate, he'd left another three pitas in his truck. He would eat them when he was finished with his pseudo-date with John. After all, it wasn't like his mate would understand his huge appetite.

I'll explain all that later. Gotta get John on board first.

"I do like the sounds you're making, John," William murmured while lifting his food to his mouth. Before taking a bite, he couldn't help but add, "And I would be *more than happy* to help you burn off those extra calories."

John froze mid-chew and stared at him with a wide-eyed expression.

William bet it took every bit of self-control John had not to gape at him. Smiling, he waggled his brows at the man he wanted to soon make his lover. "I know we're attracted to each other, John. Why do my words surprise you?"

Putting down his sandwich, John grabbed a napkin as he swallowed. He cleared his throat and wiped his hands, cleaning the drips of sauce from his fingers before it began oozing down his arms. Then he picked up his coffee mug and took a swig.

For some reason, William felt a tinge of jealousy for that cup. It was touching his mate's lips, after all. He wanted to grab his human and haul him across the desk so he could ravish his mouth. William bet John would taste fantastic.

Instead, he focused on eating, soothing his rumbling stomach.

"I don't think I've ever had anyone speak so forwardly to me before," John finally told him as he picked up his sandwich again. His hazel eyes held a hint of amusement even as his cheeks remained a lovely pinkish hue. "If we start dating, is it something I'm going to have to get used to?"

William really didn't like the *if* John had used. Growling softly, he finished his last bite of his first pita. As he wiped his hands, he pinned a hungry gaze on John.

"Oh, John," William rumbled gruffly. "There is no *if*. We are already dating. Those phone calls we've been sharing? That was us getting to know each other." Using the soiled napkin to indicate between them, he claimed, "This is our first *official* date, as unorthodox as it is, because I'm willing to work around the fact that you have family in town and need to spend most of your free time with them." William winked as he leaned over the desk. "I'm thoughtful like that. And, yeah, I'm definitely going to be sharing my desires with you. Just as I hope you'll share yours with me."

John stared back at William, holding his gaze steadily. After a few long seconds, he nodded once.

Pleasure filled William at his mate's acquiescence.

"My son and his family are leaving on Friday night," John said, although he'd already told William that. Before William could remind him of that conversation on the phone, John continued, "Are you available Saturday?"

Pleasure coursed through William. "Absolutely. Do you like fishing?"

"I do."

"Good." William unwrapped his second pita. "Then take the second exit after the one for *World of Aquatica*. I'll give you the code for the gate to our private dock. Eight o'clock work for you?"

After John had nodded, William returned to his food. Just like on the phone, they easily fell into light conversation, sharing about themselves—well, sort of on William's end. All the while William looked forward to Saturday.

Deep sea fishing on the ocean will be the perfect opportunity for alone time with my mate.

Chapter Four

John stopped his *Ford* Taurus in front of the electronic gates. After taking a deep breath, he let it out slowly. His heart pounded wildly in his chest, and sweat broke out on his temples.

Am I really doing this?

Rubbing the back of his neck, John tried to even out his breathing. He reached down and adjusted himself. Just the prospect of seeing William again had him stiffening in his jeans. John didn't understand it.

Or maybe it's the memory of his kiss. God, that had been so amazing.

The memory flashed through his mind even as he tried to think of something else.

After they'd both eaten their food — John couldn't remember the last time someone had been so thoughtful to figure out his favorite food, then to bring it to him — William rose to his feet. Without preamble, he rounded the desk while wiggling his fingers in an upward motion, indicating that John should stand.

Without thought, John obeyed. He opened his mouth to ask what William needed, but the man cradled his jaw, freezing his breath in his lungs. His other hand landed on John's hip and squeezed gently. Tingles erupted through his groin where William's thumb was so very close.

"Now, John," William rumbled softly, his tone husky and low. "I'm going to give you a goodbye kiss and miss the fuck out of you over the next few days."

John had never understood the phrase *his eyes smoldered* . . . until right then. William's green eyes definitely smoldered. John's breath caught in his chest at the intensity of that look.

"Tell me you're ready for that."

With his blood rushing through his veins in a way John couldn't ever remember feeling, he swallowed hard enough to cause his Adam's apple to bob. His prick swelled in his slacks. While he couldn't get his throat to work, John still managed to nod.

William growled softly, his green eyes glittering. As he slowly dipped his head, he held John's gaze. When his lips were a hairsbreadth from his own, and John could feel his breath against his lips, he paused.

"Say yes," William whispered, his eyes full of heat. "Say yes, John."

Unable to resist William's allure, John once again obeyed. "Yes."

Then William sealed his lips over John's own. He didn't ask. He took. William nipped at John's lower lip, drawing a gasp from him.

William tipped his head sideways, positioning his lips over John's more securely. He thrust his tongue into his mouth and lapped along John's own. Next, he pushed his tongue deeper, swirling it around John's mouth as he mapped it with single-minded intensity.

Goose bumps broke out on John's upper arms. The hairs on his nape stood on end. Tingles worked down his chest, causing his nipples to bead.

Acting on instinct and need, John grabbed William's hip with one hand. With his other, he threaded his fingers through the bigger man's hair. John gripped his hair and pushed upward into his mouth, thrusting his tongue into

William's mouth and giving as good as he got.

His mind clouded. His blood burned in his veins. His entire body felt as if fiery tingles coursed over him.

It wasn't until black spots danced across his vision and his lungs burned with his need for oxygen that he jerked his head backward. He heaved, sucking in deep, gasping breaths as he stared up the couple inches of height difference to meet William's gaze. It was a novel experience, looking up at the person he'd just kissed.

Kissed. Ha! Ravished and was ravished in return.

Easing his hand from William's hair, John realized he'd practically yanked the man's hair tie from his tail. William didn't seem to mind. Not if the way the man peered at him was anything to go by.

"So," William murmured softly, tracing his fingertips along John's jawline as he pulled away from him. His slightly puffy lips were curved into a wide grin. "As much as I want to continue, what I have in mind will cause far too much noise."

Releasing John, William took a step backward. He lifted his left hand and pulled his already loosened tie from his hair, then thrust his right through his thick, wavy black locks. After a few finger-combs, he retied his hair.

"God, that shouldn't look so sexy."

John didn't even realize he'd said the words out loud until William beamed a huge smile at him. "Thanks, John." William winked. "I think you're damn fine yourself."

"Are you going to sit out here all morning?"

John would forever deny the startled bark that escaped his throat. Gaping, he peered at William through the open window. The sexy man had his forearms resting on his hood and was bent so he could stare in at him.

When the hell did he walk up to my car?

Scowling at the man, John grumbled, "Don't do that."

William grinned, although the expression appeared a little sheepish. "Sorry, handsome. You must have been really deep in thought." Sliding his gaze down . . . and down . . . William focused on John's crotch. "And they must have been damn good thoughts." Meeting John's gaze again, William gave him a lecherous smile. "Care to share, John?"

John gathered the same courage he used to deal with reporters, forcing his pounding heart to calm. Smirking at William, he teased, "You know, I knew we were going fishing, but I thought that was later." He spotted the way William's dark brows shot up, so decided to add, "You know. On the ocean? You should have told me we were fishing on shore. I would have brought you some waders."

After an instant, William broke into a huge smile as he barked a laugh. "Touché," he replied, straightening. "Follow me down. I'll show you where to park."

Still grinning, William pushed away from John's car and strode swiftly to a golf cart.

Yep, I didn't hear that drive up, either.

John would have felt foolish, except then his focus landed on William's tall, broad form and confident movements, distracting him from his thoughts. Every step caused the muscles in his calves to flex as well as his ass, which was beautifully hugged by the dark-blue and white striped board shorts he wore. Even William's pale green tank top showcased the strong lines of his back.

It wasn't until William climbed into the golf cart, cutting off John's view, did he manage to scrape together a few brain cells.

Shaking his head at himself, John shifted his vehicle into gear and followed the golf cart as it led the way down the paved road. He drove down a fairly steep grade with a metal railing to his right and the cliff to his left. When John rounded a bend, the view opened up, revealing a nice-sized parking area, a boat ramp, and a small marina.

33

John whistled under his breath as he took in the small yacht that was docked at the farthest slip.

William stopped the golf cart in the parking area, so John did the same. He popped his trunk before exiting the vehicle. From within there, John grabbed his duffle bag and slung it over his shoulder. It contained a spare change of clothes and a jacket as well as a few snacks—a bag of granola, a canister of peanuts, and a couple of pieces of fruit.

When John reached for his fishing tackle box and his rod, William appeared next to him and touched his wrist. "You won't need that, John." He grinned as he indicated John's pole. "Not unless you have a hundred or more pound line on that thing."

Leaving his tackle box in his truck, John straightened as disbelief filled him. "A hundred pounds? Just what are we fishing for today?"

Laughing, William shrugged. "Anything you want. What if we snag an awesome eighty-five or ninety-pound tuna? Even a decent seabass could be fifty pounds." He knocked his shoulder against John's as he added, "Unless you think it's a lucky pole or something, leave it. I have everything we need."

John shrugged. "Okay." He placed the pole back inside and closed the trunk. Then he lifted his key fob and hit the lock button.

William laughed again as he hooked his arm around John's waist. After pressing a kiss to John's temple, he teased, "Who do you think is going to try to steal your ride, handsome?" William pointed toward a discreetly placed camera affixed on a ledge of a cliff at the edge of the parking lot. "Besides, any action down here gets verified as soon as it happens to keep trespassers out. Smile. You're on *Candid Camera*."

Chuckling at William's teasing tone, John nodded. "Habit.

I live in the city."

Letting out a hum, William narrowed his eyes. "Yeah. You're a little far away."

John wondered what William could mean by that, but then the man used his free hand to cradle his jaw. Even as they walked—albeit slower—William sealed his lips over John's and gave him a welcoming kiss.

When William lifted his head, he grinned down at John. He loved the scrambled-brain, glazed-eyes expression his kisses put on his mate's face. It caused his pulse to thud wildly in his chest and his heart to swell with pride.

"Come on," William urged, sliding his hand down to twine his fingers with John's. "Let's get going." He waggled his brows. "I can't wait to get you all to myself."

John chuckled, but he sped up his walk to keep pace with William. "The crowds around here making you nervous, big guy?"

Laughing, William winked at him. "Away from cameras, too." He glanced behind him, knowing Ovram—their technology expert who shared his spirit with a sea lion—was watching every move they made. "So, you're obviously comfortable kissing a man, and while I don't particularly want to discuss your past conquests, I am interested in just how much experience you have on my side of the fence." William forced a smile when he spotted the telltale color on John's cheeks, gathering his self-control so he wouldn't say something inappropriately possessive. "I don't want to freak you out by pushing too hard, John, but I want to be honest with you, too."

I want to fuck and claim you so damn bad.

William kept that thought to himself. He needed to introduce John to his animal first. After over a week of knowing the man and many words of caution and advice from not only his brother but the other mated shifters at the park, William still had no idea how he was going to accomplish that.

Maybe Fate will show me the way.

"Uh, well, I told you I married Sheila when I was still in the academy, then she left me four years later when Jonathan was two, remember?"

William nodded. "I do." He remembered everything John had ever told him.

"Well, while in high school, I fooled around with a couple of guys. We were all on the football team together." John shoved his hands into the pockets of his jeans. His face had turned a deep shade of pink, and he was staring at the yacht, obviously unwilling to meet William's gaze. "Public showers, testosterone, nudity. It started out with playful swats on the ass and went from there." Finally, John flicked his gaze toward William, but only for an instant. He snorted. "Dares, ya see." Shrugging, he finished, "Kissing a guy was just as good as any of the girls. Plus I loved the jerk circles . . . getting to see the other guys' hard dicks. The feel of their hard flesh in my palm, making them cry out." John cleared his throat, scratching the back of his neck with his left hand as he mumbled, "Heady stuff. But then I graduated." Meeting William's gaze fully, John told him seriously, "It was different in the academy back then. It wasn't all right to be . . . out. I pushed my bisexuality into a box and dated women. Got married. Had a kid. I'd never admit it to Jonathan, but Sheila leaving was a good thing for me, even if it meant working long hours and scrimping and saving, so I could raise him."

"Thank you for sharing," William responded, his tone a husky growl he couldn't hide. He hoped John thought it was from arousal and not from the jealousy coursing through his system. Teasing his fingertips along his mate's temple, tracing the gray hairs there, William told him, "Soon, I'm gonna get your cherry, and you will be mine."

John's nostrils flared as he sucked in a harsh breath. His

lips parted a little, and his tongue slipped out to wet them. "Sure of yourself, are you?" he whispered, his voice sounding breathy.

William scented John's arousal, the masculine aroma perfuming the air and making his mouth water. "Of you, absolutely," he replied gruffly. "I've wanted you since the second we met." Threading the fingers of his free hand into John's hair, he teased along the back of his scalp. "You draw me as no other ever has, and I know we can be great together."

From the way John's jaw sagged open, William realized he might have been a little too forward. He refused to backtrack, however. While he hadn't planned to blurt out declarations quite yet, what was done was done.

Damn. Guess my patience is wearing thinner than I thought.

"Left you a little shocked, I guess." William shrugged, then pressed a kiss to the corner of John's mouth. After that, he slid the tips of his fingers from where he'd been caressing his mate's temple down under his chin. As he used them to urge John to close his mouth, William told him, "There's no point beating around the bush, John. I've been waiting for a connection like the one we have for a very, *very* long time. Now come on. Let's go have some fun."

William released John after another too short peck to the lips he loved to taste. "Come on."

Leading the way down the long dock to the small yacht, William guided John onto it. He and Kaiser used it when they wanted to head to deeper water for big game hunting in squid form. While it wasn't required that they eat while an animal, it definitely pleased their other half.

Besides, William found it fun and great exercise. He knew his brother used it to blow off steam.

William showed John around the large craft, then fired up the engine. After he'd unhooked her lines from the dock, he guided the yacht along a carefully dug channel that could accommodate its deeper draw. As they headed to open sea,

William reveled in the wide grin on John's face.

He hoped what he intended to share while he had John as a captive audience wouldn't cause his mate's happiness to flee.

CHAPTER FIVE

John laughed as William reeled in another fish. Somehow, the man seemed to have a sixth sense as to where they would be as well as what kind. William changed the bait often, explaining to John what each bait was designed to attract.

For a few seconds, John admired the large seabass William was landing. The yank on his pole returned his attention back to his own line. He jerked upward, then began fighting to reel in his strike.

Bracing against his chair's harness, John was damn glad for the security it provided. He could imagine himself being yanked right into the ocean without it. His arm muscles strained as did his legs and abdominals. Never had John thought of fishing as a full-body workout until that morning.

"You got it, John! Keep tugging," William encouraged. "At this rate, we'll have enough to feed us for a week."

"A week?" John barked a laugh, then gritted his teeth as the fish on the other end of the line gave an extra vigorous tug. Still, John couldn't help glancing at William before refocusing on reeling in his fish. "We've already caught like . . . eight huge fish. How can you say just a week?"

William leaned close, nuzzling his nose along John's neck. "I have a big appetite, John," he whispered, his warm breath fanning over the hairs behind John's ear.

John jolted, nearly dropping his pole. "Shit," he hissed, glancing over his shoulder for just a second. "You keep doing that and you're gonna make me drop this pole."

Even as William chuckled, he straightened a little, putting a few inches between them. "I've lost my fair share of poles out here," he admitted. He rested his hands on John's shoulders and massaged lightly. "Almost there. I can see a dark body moving in the water."

John pressed into his touch, loving William's touchy-feely-ness. During the course of the morning, he'd done a lot of it, too. William would brush his fingers over his neck, up his spine, and over his shoulder. Just as often William paused to dip his head and press a kiss to John's skin . . . and it wasn't just his lips. His neck, nape, temple, and even his ear had been thoroughly mapped by William's lips.

For the first time in several decades, John's body was thrumming with a steady beat of arousal. At first, he'd been confused about what William was doing, since he never went beyond that. It had taken John over an hour to figure it out.

William is getting me used to his touch.

It was a spine-tingling and ball-rolling experience, and John loved every damn second of it.

Maybe I need to do a little touching of my own.

Grinning at his idea, John finally managed to spot the fish William had claimed he'd seen. As they'd been at it, John had discovered his date had extremely amazing eyesight. Plus he was strong, making reeling in the big fish he continued to catch look so damn easy.

Watching William's muscles ripple — the man was wearing a pale-green tank top that showed off his torso nearly to perfection — made John's mouth water. He wanted to rip the thin fabric from the man so he could see the rest of him. More than once, John had felt his fingers twitch with his desires.

So what the fuck am I waiting for?

For the first time in John's life, he had every intention of taking what he wanted.

"Come on, John," William urged. "Focus, or you're gonna lose it. You tired?" He rubbed his palms down John's back. "You need me to take it?"

Right. Focus on the damn fish.

"I'm okay. Almost got it." John smirked over his shoulder at William for a second, saying, "Get ready with the hook to catch it."

William did as John had instructed, getting ready to help John land the fish.

Once they'd gotten it in the boat, William grinned broadly at him as the small tuna flopped on the deck. "That's a damn nice one, John." He grabbed the fillet knife and stabbed it through the big fish's brain, ending its life with swift precision. "I think we're gonna eat this one. You about ready for lunch?"

As if on cue, John's stomach growled.

Chuckling, William cast a grin his way. "Good answer, my handsome mate." He winked at him, then asked, "Will you start putting the fishing gear back together while I fillet this seventy pound beast you brought in? Then I'll gut the seabass I landed and start cooking."

"Gonna make me lunch, big man," John teased with a grin even as he obeyed and began working on the cleaning up their gear.

"Of course." William snickered deeply as he winked at John. "The way to a man's heart is through his stomach, after all."

At that, John felt said heart skip a beat. *William wants my heart?* As he replayed over all their interactions, John could definitely see how everything the man did was moving them in that direction.

Pulling himself out of his thoughts, John finished cleaning up their supplies. He was done long before William was, so he made himself at home in the galley. Finding a baking sheet, olive oil, and even several different kinds of seasonings, John laid everything out on the counter.

John didn't know how William intended to prepare the fish, but he knew they had way more meat than needed. "A week," he mumbled, remembering the almost dozen large fish that they'd already caught. "He thinks he can eat all that in a week?"

"Well, you, me, and my brother," William stated, entering the room. He grinned widely as he waggled his brows. "The large appetites will make sense after lunch."

While John didn't understand the man's comment, he nodded anyway. He watched William place the fillets on the baking sheet. Noticing the blood on the younger man's hands, John turned on the kitchen faucet.

God, the conveniences on this thing.

William flashed a grin his way, then crossed to it and began washing his hands.

Taking advantage of William's distraction, John slipped behind him. He brazenly rested his hands on the man's sides, then eased his palms under the hem of his tank top. Goose bumps broke out on his forearms as he rubbed over William's firm back muscles.

William froze for a second, then hummed as he peered over his shoulder at John. His expression was one of pleasure. Heat lit up his eyes.

"Playing with fire, John," William rumbled.

Damn the man is ripped.

John didn't understand what the man saw in him, but he seemed so damn sure of what he wanted.

I intend to take advantage of that for as long as possible.

Even knowing it was the cheesiest thing he'd ever said, John met William's hungry gaze while replying hotly, "And what if I want to get burned?"

William's eyes narrowed, and he appeared extremely pleased. "Then touch away."

For the first time in a long, *long* time, John did what he

wanted without care for what was best for everyone else. He pushed William's shirt upward, admiring every tanned, toned stretch of skin as he did so. John traced over the grooves of William's muscles, the knobs of his spine, and even the delineation of his ribs. Everything on the man spoke of masculine beauty and perfection.

John lowered his gaze and focused on William's ass behind the fabric of his striped shorts.

I want a piece of that.

Lowering his hands, John gripped William's globes. He felt the clench of the firm mounds, while at the same time, a rumbling growl erupted from William's chest and a tremble worked through the bigger man's body. A shiver of power coursed through John, knowing he'd caused such a reaction in the larger man.

Hell yeah!

William trembled where he stood. Only by gripping the edge of the sink did he manage to keep from turning around and grabbing his mate. The feel of John sliding his palms over his back, tracing his spine, and sliding around his sides caused the hairs on his nape to stand on end. His squid vocalized low in his mind, and his body thrummed with need.

Groaning softly, William shuddered. "Gods, John. Does just the idea of me cooking fish for lunch get you hot?" He peered over his shoulder and met John's gaze, knowing his hunger showed clearly in his eyes. "Or have you run out of patience? You know you can do anything to me you want."

"Anything?" John asked breathily. He held William's gaze even as he continued to massage William's ass cheeks, pulling them apart, then allowing them to ease back together again.

William's channel clenched. He knew what John wanted, and while he hadn't bottomed in over two centuries, he would for his mate. He curved his lips into a feral grin. *"Anything."*

John's nostrils flared, and his eyes dilated. He swallowed so hard his Adam's apple bobbed. Groaning, he grabbed the base of William's shirt and tugged upward.

Happy to go along with his encouragement, William lifted his arms as he bent sideways at the waist. He growled softly, reveling in the fact that his mate was undressing him. Once John had whipped it over his head and off his hands, William turned to face John.

William rested both his rear and his hands on the counter behind him, flexing his pectorals invitingly. "Now what, my mate?"

He mentally winced at the slip. He knew it wasn't the first time he'd used it. Fortunately, John seemed too interested in admiring him to notice.

"Now —" John's stomach grumbled.

Fighting back a wince, William crooked his lips into a half-smile. "How about you ditch your shirt and jeans so I can admire the view while I feed you?" William spotted the disappointment in John's eyes. Lifting his left hand, he cradled his mate's jaw in his palm as he assured, "We're not stopping, John. Not by a long shot. However" — sliding his second hand to his human's waist, feeling the hint of softness there — "what I want us to share requires plenty of energy, and I don't want to rush because of hunger."

William saw the acceptance in John's eyes as well as the flair of renewed desire. "Then you better get cooking." Stepping backward, he grabbed the hem of his shirt, then hesitated. John tipped his chin toward William's body. "I'm older than you William, and I don't look like that anymore."

Even as William understood the warning — and mentally laughed at his *older than you* comment — he kept his facial features in a reassuring smile. "Oh, handsome. You don't need to worry about that." William rested his hand on John's shoulder, then slid his palm down his chest to his mate's belly. "I know I'm going to love your body just as it is. Please don't be concerned about that."

John shivered under William's touch, his stomach muscles fluttering. After clearing his throat, he nodded. When John began lifting his shirt, William pulled his hands away to give him room.

A growl of appreciation and approval rumbled from William's throat. His gaze gobbled up all the smooth, pale lines of John's torso. He wanted to tweak John's pale nipples and lick and nip every inch of his lightly haired flesh between them. William would map his mate's smooth, flat belly so John would never fear his attraction to his man.

After John had dropped the shirt to the floor, he reached for the fly of his jeans. Pausing, he met William's gaze. "What about you?" John flicked his gaze toward William's groin before focusing back on his face. "You gonna ditch the shorts, too?"

William couldn't help the feral quality he knew filled his grin. "Oh, handsome." Stepping forward, he rested his hands on John's upper arms and nuzzled his nose against the crook of the man's neck. When his mate tipped his head, William's mouth filled with water as his body flooded with the urge to bite him. "I go commando, John. Is that okay with you?"

John's breathing hitched. He shivered within William's grip. "C-Commando."

Oh, that breathy moan filling his words is a thing of beauty. Want to hear that sound again and again . . . forever.

"Yep." William nipped at the flesh he longed to mark. "I'm a free-baller." Realizing there were occasional exceptions to that, he added, "Unless I'm going to one of those damn charity auctions and have to wear a tux." William lifted his head and met John's gaze, pleased to see the arousal flushing his features. "Then I wear briefs."

Surprisingly, John smirked. "You gonna brave the stove without any clothes on?"

"I told you. For you" — William winked — "anything."

John laughed, his hazel eyes twinkling. "Maybe you should put an apron on. Is there one around here?" He pulled away and began looking around the galley with interest, a grin still lighting his features. "Then I could still sit around admiring your ass."

William barked a laugh and nodded. "I think that's a fair compromise." Without waiting a second longer, he gripped the elastic waist of his board shorts and pulled it forward, then down, revealing his thick erection. As he pushed the shorts down his legs and pulled them off, lifting each foot in turn, William leered at his mate. "Better hurry up, John. There's a lot I want to do to you."

John whimpered — the sound causing William's dick to twitch — but he got moving.

By the time William straightened and set his shorts on a nearby chair, John had unbuttoned and unzipped his jeans. William watched with anticipation as his mate's green boxer-briefs were revealed, but he didn't get a chance to look for long since John immediately bent, pushing down the material. He enjoyed the view of John's nicely muscled legs, then when his mate straightened, William practically swallowed his tongue.

All thought of waiting flew from his mind as he took in the view of John's erection tenting his underwear. There was already a small damp spot on the fabric. The need to taste overruled every good intention or patient brain cell that he had left.

Dropping to his knees, William rested his hands on John's hips. He teased his fingertips into the fabric of his mate's briefs even as he nuzzled his cheek along John's covered erection. Inhaling deeply, William relished the deep masculine aromas wafting from his soon-to-be lover.

"Can I suck you, John?" William figured he should at least ask.

John groaned. His fingers threaded into William's hair. His hips popped forward spastically as if he were fighting his urges.

"D-Don't think it's gonna matter if you suck me or not," John rasped. "I-I'm gonna—" He broke off on another moan.

Unwilling to resist the chance to taste John's seed, William swiftly eased the fabric down. He let out a moan of his own upon the view revealed to him. John's cock was maybe seven inches and thick—a perfect mouthful. Pre-cum gleamed at the tip, and his crown was already damp.

"W-William!"

Loving the needy way John called his name, William gave him what he wanted. He opened his mouth and swallowed his mate's dick to the root. His human's slightly salty, masculine flavor burst across his tongue, making his taste buds sing and flooding his senses.

William's cock throbbed as he enjoyed the tang of John's pre-cum on his tongue. He sucked strongly, pulling partway off. Hearing John's cry, feeling his dick twitch in his mouth as more pre-cum dripped onto his tongue, William knew his mate hadn't been lying.

My gorgeous needy mate.

Sucking strongly, William rubbed his tongue along John's length, massaging it. At the same time, he cupped his balls, rolling them ever-so-gently.

John roared and bucked. His hold tugged at William's hair, making his scalp tingle. The sensation transferred straight to his own cock, and his length twitched and jerked where it jutted heavily from his groin.

When John's seed burst from his human, coating William's tongue, he let out a moan of his own. His lover's flavor—lightly salted and rich—reminding William of his favorite sardines—sent a fiery blast to go hurtling through his veins. It settled in his groin.

As William drank down his mate's heady fluids, his own orgasm swamped his senses. Groaning in bliss around his mouthful, he shuddered with his pleasure. He couldn't remember the last time he'd come untouched and was loving every second of it.

So fucking perfect.

CHAPTER SIX

John sat on the booth seat in his underwear, watching William sauté the tuna fillets. He rested his forearms on the table before him and tried to swallow down his embarrassment. After all, William wore nothing at all.

He hadn't found an apron, although John suspected the man hadn't looked very hard.

Even after coming twenty minutes before—they'd spent that time putting away the rest of the tuna and seabass meat from their recent catches—John still sported a half-hard prick. He also had to keep his focus on William's movements. If his gaze fell to William's naked ass or hard dick, which he seemed completely comfortable showing off, John knew that he, too, would end up with another boner. John couldn't remember the last time he'd recovered so fast.

"Something on your mind, John?" William asked, glancing his way.

John realized he must have done something to give away his discomfort. Sighing, he gave in to temptation and openly ogled William's naked form. His lips curved into a wry smile as his own body responded to the amazing view.

With a deep sigh, John leaned back on the bench seat. He even spread his legs a little so he could adjust his erection into a more comfortable position. Waving at his groin, John shrugged.

"I can't remember the last time I've gotten a boner twice in one evening let alone within thirty minutes of each other," John stated, shifting his weight a little so his balls didn't ache. "I'm fifty-one years old, William. This shouldn't be possible."

William swept his gaze over John, his grin turning lecherous. "You complaining? I sure as hell ain't." He pointed his spatula at John. "You'd probably be more comfortable without those on."

"No way was I gonna use a fillet knife while my bits were swinging in the wind," John grumbled.

"And now?" William pressed, glancing meaningfully at his own groin. "I'd really like you to be as comfortable as I am."

John rubbed the back of his neck, then heaved a sigh. "When in Rome," he muttered before lifting his hips and using both hands to shove his underwear under his butt. As John shimmied them off his legs and carelessly kicked them away, he grumbled, "What the fuck is it with you that I can't get sex off the brain?" Taking a chance, John admitted, "Ever since I met you I've wanted to fuck your ass, William."

William's nostrils flared, and he pinned a heated gaze on John. "I will welcome that, John." Then his eyes narrowed. "Just as I'll make you cry out with ecstasy when I fuck *your* ass, my handsome mate."

John cocked his head, realizing William had used that word a few times. When his new lover cleared his throat and went back to fixing up the food, he realized it might have been a slip of the tongue. He wondered if it had some kind of meaning.

"These are done. As are the vegetables," William stated, pulling two plates from a cupboard over his head. After placing them on the counter, he checked the rice. "Ah, perfect. So's the rice."

William prepared the plates—fresh, lemon and herbed tuna on a bed of wild rice, along with a large portion of yellow squash and zucchini chunks. On top of all of it, William drizzled a healthy dollop of lobster gravy. When the big man placed the plates on the table, John noticed that—as William had claimed—he had made his own plate twice the size of John's.

"There's plenty more in the pans, John," William told him, obviously noticing that John had noticed the discrepancy. He grinned as he waggled his brows. "I told you I have a big appetite."

"This is plenty for me, I'm sure," John replied, shaking his head. "And I have no idea how you can eat all that and stay in such amazing shape."

William beamed at him as he stabbed his fork into his food.

John followed suit. He found the tuna flaked perfectly around his fork. The dressing was rich and flavorful. The flavors mixed wonderfully with the fish and rice. Even the vegetables were perfectly cooked.

"Oh, wow," John mumbled. He had to remind himself to chew thoroughly, or he would have shoveled the food into his mouth like a heathen. "So damn good."

Outside of a restaurant, John couldn't remember the last time he'd tasted a fish meal so amazing. *Had a restaurant tasted this wonderful?* John wasn't certain.

William obviously appreciated his enthusiasm, for his smile was filled with smug satisfaction. He didn't comment, however. Instead, he focused on gobbling up his own meal.

"We should be slowing down and savoring this exquisite food you prepared," John lamented even as he stabbed his fork into a couple of pieces of zucchini and swirled it through the lobster sauce. "But I can't help it. It's too good."

"I don't mind at all, John. And I'll make it for you again, so you can savor it later." William leaned forward, staring at him with desire darkening his deep green eyes. "Just think, the faster we eat, the sooner we get to round two."

John needed no further prodding. He couldn't remember the last time he'd thought with his dick, but he sure was right then. As much as the food tasted beyond wonderful, John wanted sex even more.

Just as William claimed, he managed to eat all his food. In fact, he was even done at the same time as John. William pushed his plate away, then he stood and held out his hand.

"Let's retreat to the cabin, John. The dishes will wait."

Anticipation thrumming through John, causing his hard dick to leak a bead of pre-cum, he took William's hand. His lover drew him up and, with a sharp tug, pulled him flush against him. The heat of William's body coupled with the feel of hard flesh against his own, drew a moan from his throat.

"I fucking love the noises you make," William stated on a growl before he dipped his head and captured John's lips.

William nipped John's bottom lip, then thrust his tongue in deep. He tangled their appendages together, teasing and stimulating him. His hand gripped John's hip, encouraging him to rock his hips and rub against him.

John groaned into William's mouth. Clutching at the bigger man's shoulders, he rutted unashamedly. Everything about William caused his blood to boil in a way he'd never before experienced. With the way William not only openly accepted but encouraged his responses, John found his normal self-control shot to hell.

Feeling his balls begin to churn and more pre-cum ooze from his erection, John jerked backward.

William immediately released him, his expression questioning.

"Bedroom," John gasped out. "N-Now."

Growling, William jerked a nod. "Hell yeah."

After pivoting, William stalked around the dining booth and through a back door.

John followed, his gaze riveting to the exquisite flexing globes of William's ass. He watched as his lover pulled open a nightstand, drawing out a tube of lubricant. When William crawled onto the bed on his hands and knees, putting his ass on display, John sucked in a harsh breath and finally met the other man's face.

Seeing the feral desire filling William's deep green eyes, John moaned and gripped the base of his dick. He couldn't believe how close he was to coming again. John had no clue how he was going to touch his lover, to do what needed to be done, and not spill his seed.

William easily seemed to pick up on his predicament. Grinning widely, he popped the cap off the lube and poured some onto his fingers. He used his thumb to close it and tossed it aside before reaching behind himself.

Resting his weight on his left forearm, William sank his middle finger into his ass. He eased it out, then pushed it in again. On the next pull out and push in, William added a second finger.

John's breath caught in his throat. Climbing onto the bed, he gripped the base of his dick in a tight hold. He groaned as he stared at where William prepared himself for his taking.

"W-William, I—" John squeezed his dick tighter. He couldn't believe how ramped up he was.

What the fuck is wrong with me?

But then William pulled his fingers free and levered onto his knees.

"Come here, handsome," William encouraged, his voice gruff. "Come here so I can grease up your pole, then I want to feel you deep."

Even as John knee-walked forward, drawing closer to William, something flitted in the back of his mind. Then his lover's lube-slicked fingers wrapped around his erection, and all thought fled. John gasped harshly as William's lightly calloused fingers slid up and down his length, causing sparks of sensation to zing down his dick to his balls.

"Oh fuck!" John bucked into the hold, his aching cock desperate for friction. "William!"

"Line up, John," William urged, releasing him. He shifted a little on the bed so John was between his spread legs, his ass on beautiful display before him. "I want you, John. Please give it to me."

William begging for his cock sent fire coursing through John's veins. A primal need to bury himself as deeply into his needy lover took over, his instincts screaming at him to obey. Positioning his crown at William's stretched hole, John thrust.

In one long glide, John sank his erection deep into William's body. His lover's chute muscles rippled along his length, offering the most delicious massage. Buried deep, John froze.

John gasped as he struggled to keep his balls from unloading while he assimilated the most amazing ecstasy of his life.

"Oh god," John whined, shuddering hard. "I never wanna leave."

John hadn't meant to say that out loud, but William's next words told him he didn't seem to mind—not one little bit.

"You feel perfect."

William groaned roughly, reveling in the feel of being connected to his mate. At the same time, he did his best to relax his chute muscles. His channel felt stretched to capacity, even though William knew John wasn't what most would call oversized.

To me, though, he's perfect.

When John started moving, his flared crown sliding along William's inner muscles, goose bumps broke out on his thighs. His spine tingled, and his balls ached. William knew he wasn't long in coming.

Hell, lunch had been the most erotic form of foreplay, and all they'd been doing was eating.

William felt John's fingernails digging into his sides. He heard his mate's soft grunts—his noises betraying his excitement. The pricks at his sides coupled with the lightly burning stretch to his chute caused William's ecstasy to skyrocket.

With his cock leaking like a sieve, William knew he was seconds away from coming. His tingling spine and tightening testicles caused a shudder to roll through him. Clenching around John's erection each time his mate pulled out, William urged his lover to come with him.

"Will!" John cried as he sank deep.

Feeling his mate's warm seed splash over his insides, William groaned in bliss. He stopped fighting. His balls tightened, and he came, growling his mate's name.

William's senses buzzed out. His mind swam as ecstasy crashed through him, pulling him under like a riptide. His arms gave out, and he flopped forward, sinking onto the comforter.

When William slowly regained his senses, he had his head cradled in one arm. At some point he couldn't remember, he'd moved his left arm behind so he could grip John's hip. William felt the heavy weight of his mate sprawled over his back, and to his pleasure, his human's softened prick still stretched his body.

"Damn, John," William mumbled. He peered over his shoulder and spotted John staring down at him with one bleary-looking eye. His other eye was closed. "Can't ever remember feeling so good."

While William knew John still didn't understand why their attraction was so intense, he relished the sated smile John graced him with. Even feeling the dampness against his belly and realizing he lay in the wet spot couldn't diminish William's joy. He loved the headway they were making.

Now if only our relationship will survive the truth of me and shifters.

After several minutes of lying sprawled over his back, William finally felt John shift above him. His mate groaned as he eased his softened dick from William's body. William smiled as he watched a relaxed looking John flop to the right of him.

Wanting out of the wet spot—and since the bed was a king size with plenty of room—William wrapped his arm around John's waist. He eased closer to his mate, moving him a little as he went. Once the dampness no longer cooled him, William slid his left arm under John's head and cuddled him close.

William heaved a huge sigh as endorphins continued to ping through his system. Unfortunately, his lethargy couldn't completely take over, because he felt a hint of tension in John's body. Maybe his mate wasn't a cuddler.

Hopefully, I can change that.

Rubbing his palm up and down John's side, William pressed a kiss to his mate's temple. "What has you thinking so hard over there?"

John turned his head and met William's gaze fully. "We didn't use a condom." His brows furrowed, and there was a hint of tightness around his lips. "I, uh, I'm clean. On the force we get tested regularly, but, uh—" John seemed to run out of steam.

Along with John's rambling, which betrayed his unease, William read something else from John's scent.

Uncertainty. Concern. Even a little fear.

Well, damn. That wasn't what I hoped for after sex.

On the other hand, William decided maybe starting the *I'm a paranormal* talk while lying wrapped up in post-coital bliss and in each other's arms would be a good thing.

56

"I don't have anything, either," William decided to start with. "And you're the first human I've ever done anything with without a condom."

William paused, wondering if John would take the bait.

"I'm sorry." John's brows shot up. "Did you just say, first *human*?"

Good.

Nodding, William slid his palm up and traced over John's chest. "I did." He decided to use the rip off the band-aid approach and see where things fell. "I'm what's called a shifter. A type of paranormal. I share my spirit with an animal, and I can change into my other form at will." As William spoke, he saw the way John's eyes began to narrow and how his features tightened. He scoffed softly as he teased up to slide his fingers over his shoulder. "There are far more creatures than just humans on Earth, my mate."

When John pulled away, William loosened his grip. He'd expected the move, but that didn't mean he didn't like it any less. His squid writhed uncomfortably in the back of his mind, and William agreed.

No, I will never let this man go. No matter what. I will make him understand.

Levering up onto his elbow, John didn't go far. He scowled down at William. "Look. Sexual safety is important. This isn't some laughing matter where you make up stories to—"

William rested his fingertips over John's lips, ceasing his angry tirade. The action earned him a growl. His mate's angry scent washed over him.

"I promise I'm clean, John, and that's not what this is," William assured him. "I can prove every word I say."

John snorted, his lips curving down in annoyance.

Remaining undeterred, William pointed out, "You wondered why your body responded so swiftly to mine. Why you couldn't seem to get enough of me. The answer is simple." His heart hammering in his chest, William prayed to the gods that his next words wouldn't send John over the tipping point. "I'm a shifter. You're my mate, the other half of my soul. The single person living on this planet who completes me . . . just as I complete you." Giving John a soft smile, William stated earnestly, "John, my mate, we were made for each other."

CHAPTER SEVEN

John gaped down at William. He couldn't believe what he was hearing. He was also having a hard time believing that William — a man who seemed so down to earth and kind — would spew such nonsense.

Why would he do such a thing? What could he possibly have to gain?

Then William's words about them being soul mates struck him. Heaving a sigh, John pushed to a sitting position. As he moved, he felt the traces of not only his seed, but the lubricant William had used to slick them both up.

His cheeks heated.

Pushing aside the reaction, John shifted his legs so his right leg was bent while still flat on the bed. It was no time for shyness, seeing as they'd already seen everything each of them had to offer. With that in mind, he stretched his left leg out straight for balance.

"I thought I already agreed that we were dating," John began slowly, sweeping his gaze over William's face. Taking in his lover's features, he tried to figure out the man's motives. "There's no need to make up wild stories to get me to agree to another date." Then another thought struck. "Are you on meds? Or, uh . . . are there meds you *should* be on but skipped taking?"

William actually chuckled as he too sat up. Resting his weight on his right hand, he rubbed his left hand over John's bent knee. "No, handsome. No meds. No drugs. Just the truth." His smile appeared a little sad as he continued, "I know you don't believe me. Humans never do without proof. So" — he began scooting toward the edge of the bed — "I'll show you." William paused once he'd lowered his legs to the floor of the yacht. "Just keep one thing in mind, okay? When I change into my animal, I'm still completely cognizant. I know exactly who you are and what you mean to me."

John didn't know what to say to that. William actually seemed certain that he could change into an animal.

Holding out his hand, palm up, William wiggled his fingers. "Care to see how deep the rabbit hole goes, Alice?"

Rolling his eyes, John took William's hands. "Sure, man. You a werewolf?" he asked, his voice dripping with sarcasm.

To John's surprise, William grinned broadly while laughing. "Not at all, my mate." He winked as he led the way out of the bedroom and back toward deck. "I'm something *a lot* bigger than a wolf, and I sure as hell don't need the full moon to change."

John just shook his head in disbelief. "How could a grown man believe in such things?"

William strode out on deck, relaxed in his nakedness.

John glanced around uneasily first. Public nudity was against the law, after all.

Winking, William squeezed John's hand. "After you believe, you tell me how you'd answer that."

Shaking his head, John opened his mouth to tell him . . . something. His thoughts ground to a halt when he saw William grab the railing and vault over the side. John stood frozen for all of two seconds . . . until he heard the sound of William's body hitting the water.

John rushed to the edge. Gripping the railing, he peered over the edge. "William?" he cried, searching the sea. A second later, his lover's head popped above the waves, the man whipping his head around to clear his thick black hair from his eyes. John glared at the man who was most definitely certifiable. "What the fuck are you doing? Where's this yacht's rope ladder. I'll throw it down to you."

William just laughed again and shook his head.

Yep. Certifiable.

"You wanted to see. I'll show you."

"Maybe you should tell me what you supposedly turn into, William," John told him. Leaning against the railing, he added, "You know. Just so I'm not scared, you being so much bigger than a wolf."

"Good point." William grinned up at him, treading water. Even with the waves nearly swamping his head with each undulation, he looked completely at home in the water. "I'm a giant squid."

"A giant, uh, g-giant squid?" John cocked his head. "Huh?"

William just continued to smile. "You'll see. Ready?"

John nodded, even though he wasn't. It sounded ludicrous.

"Remember, I will always know who you are." With those last words, William lifted his arms above his head.

Even as John wondered what to expect — *should I go search for a life preserver to throw in* — he spotted something odd. William's arms were . . . changing. John gasped when their color darkened to a greenish-gray, then split in two. Four slender limbs waved above the water from William's shoulders. Then the man sank into the sea.

"W-William?" John would forever deny the squeak in his voice. After swallowing hard, he called louder, "William?"

A low moaning bellow, which reminded him a little of a humpback whale's song, filled the air. Then a long tentacle rose from the sea, followed by a second. The appendages wrapped around the railing of the boat to John's left, but the boat didn't tip.

Even as John backed away, he realized the octopus wasn't

pulling at the yacht . . . just using it for balance.

What a weird thing to think! Wait, that second pair of tentacles look different. Right . . . William had said a giant squid.

"O-Okay . . . okay . . . um, that means—" John forced his brain to process what he was looking at—a squid— otherwise he feared he'd mentally shut down. He had a funny idea that would be bad for both of them. "There are eight arms and two feeding tentacles." Peering into the water, John gaped upon spotting the massive creature's body floating at the surface. The squid stared at him unblinkingly with one massive gray eye. "Oh my god. William?"

Movement ten feet in front of John caught his attention. As he watched the longer, slenderer appendages slide across the deck, slowly moving toward him, he backed up a step. The appendages stopped, twitching a little where they rested.

Unable to help himself, John returned his focus to the huge cephalopod floating beside the boat. "William?" John couldn't help asking again.

The creature vocalized softly—something John hadn't even realized they had the ability to do. Or was it a shifter thing? John made a mental note to ask William sometime.

"Can I touch you?" The words were out of John's mouth before he even realized he'd thought them.

Holy fucking shit! Am I believing this?

The squid made that same haunting sing-song noise.

Deciding in for a penny, in for a pound, John slowly crept toward the tentacles which still sprawled across the deck. His fingers twitched, and his heart hammered in his throat. When he stretched out his hand, it trembled.

What if I'm wrong? What if this is some wild animal that has already eaten William and is getting ready to pull me into the sea as his next course?

John scoffed at his thoughts. As quickly as they entered his mind, he realized how ridiculous they were.

No way would a giant squid be this close to the surface, let alone behave this way. While I don't know how it's possible, and I can scarcely believe it, somehow, someway . . . this squid is William. And he can understand me.

Another thought struck.

I guess it's human hubris to think we're the only things to possibly be living on this planet.

With that resolved in his mind, John rested his fingertips on the tentacle lightly. He glided his hands upward a few inches, shocked at the smoothness of the grayish skin. The appendage trembled under his touch, but it made no move to wrap around him at all.

"Holy fucking shit," John whispered in awe. His head swam a little as his world shifted under his feet—and it wasn't the rocking of the boat. John held onto the railing tightly as he straightened and peered into the sea. The squid remained right where he'd last seen it, drifting alongside the boat, patient as could be. "Shifters are real. And I'm fucking one."

That meant everything else William had told him was true, too.

"And William is my soul mate."

While John hadn't said the words loud, they must have been loud enough. The squid vocalized again as another arm slid up the side of the boat. John tensed but didn't move away as William's squid slid the back of his arm down his thigh. Every sucker flexed and contracted with the movement, but never once did they come close to John's skin.

John didn't know what to say, so he just stood there and waited. Even though he had a million questions rattling around in his head, he didn't see the point of asking them to a squid. It didn't matter that William had said he recognized John and understood while in that form. It wasn't as if the huge beast could answer back.

After what felt like an eternity to John but was probably

only five minutes, the squid pulled its limbs away from the boat. They disappeared beneath the waves, as did the huge body they were attached to. John stared into the depths, searching for any sign of a human William.

As soon as his lover's head popped over the water, John burst out, "I have so many damn questions."

"I'll tell you anything you want to know," William assured his mate.

William was beyond thrilled that John had accepted his squid so easily. He figured there was a reason his human was a police captain. John was strong and brave and made of sterner stuff — physically and mentally — than the average man.

Maybe he's more open-minded due to all the shit he must see on the street.

Allowing the change to partially slide through him, William's arm split into two squid arms. It wasn't easy, and few shifters could manage it, but he and Kaiser had worked hard to hone the ability. The move also made his arms long and slender with suckers, so he could easily climb back onto the yacht.

Just as William wrapped his arms around the railing and began reeling himself upward, the vibration of a boat motor caught his attention. He quickly eased over the railing, then strode past John. Lifting a finger in a *just a sec* gesture, William peered across the waves.

William spotted a good-sized craft speeding across the ocean . . . and it was heading straight for them. Squinting, he searched for identifying marks. There was a very slim chance that Kaiser needed him for something. However, since his brother knew William intended to share his nature with John, he was more apt to come to him in squid form and tap against the side of the boat.

"What's up?"

Without taking his attention from the approaching boat, William wrapped his arm around John's naked waist. "Looks like company. Ah, fuck," he muttered, finally able to read a logo on the side of the boat. "That's a boat owned by Perisource Enterprises. *Armando's* company. Let's go get dressed."

As William guided John back to the galley where they'd ditched their clothes, his mate commented, "Well, that was about as snide as I've ever heard you. You have a beef with Perisource? Or Armando?"

"Since they're pretty much one and the same, just like Aquatica and the Roush brothers are one and the same, both," William explained, yanking on his board shorts.

William couldn't help but hum appreciatively and slide his hand over John's ass as he bent to pull on his jeans. Smiling upon hearing his mate's grunt as he jolted, nearly falling, William wrapped his arm around John to steady him.

"I'd say sorry, but that would be a lie," William teased when John frowned at him. He knew there was no true ire in his man. "Anyway, Armando is dirty. And not just because he uses male call boys to slake his lust, and then tried to have his own son sent to somewhere to make a *real man* out of him." William curled his lip into a snarl as he thought about it, not surprised to see and scent John's surprise when he pulled away to put on his shirt. "Anyway, there's absolutely no good reason for a Perisource boat to be heading this way." Gripping John's upper arm, he leveled a serious look at his mate. "If push comes to shove, there's a loaded revolver in the port side nightstand of the bedroom. I know you know how to protect yourself, so do it. Got it?"

John's jaw sagged open, the spicy scent of his shock permeating the cabin.

"Promise me," William pressed.

"Of course." Then John's lips curved into a wry smile. "But I'll use my own gun, thanks." He pointed toward his bag which rested on a padded recliner in front of an entertainment system.

Barking a laugh, William felt his heart buoy with his joy at having John as his mate. "You're amazing," he crooned before dipping his head and pecking a hard kiss to his man's lips.

William released John and headed back to the deck.

"You're just wearing your shorts?" John questioned, dropping into step with him.

Shrugging, William told him, "If I need to shift, less to take off."

"If you need to shift? Why would you—you're expecting trouble?"

William nodded, appreciating how quick-witted John was. He didn't require a lot of explanations. Of course, William knew he still owed his mate a few about paranormals and what it meant to be his mate, but that would come soon enough.

Just as William hit the deck, he felt the telltale bump of another boat nuzzling against his yacht.

A man in a black, long-sleeved shirt and camo pants hopped onto his deck. The stranger wore a holstered sidearm on his hip. As the man grabbed the rope another man tossed him so he could tie their ships together, William leaned against the railing and scowled at those in the boat.

"It's customary to ask permission before boarding another person's boat," William commented mildly. As soon as John drew close enough, he wrapped his arm around his lover. His instinct to keep the man safe rode him hard . . . especially in the presence of all those guns. "What do you want, Stiles?"

William directed his question at Stiles Gribble. He knew

the big, black man was Armando's right-hand man and the head of his security. That he was here with three gunmen didn't bode well for their visit.

Stiles crossed his arms over his broad, t-shirt-covered chest. His smile held a cold, reptilian quality. "I'd hoped to catch you alone, but one casualty isn't going to make me lose sleep." Flicking his fingers at John—a man he obviously didn't recognize—Stiles ordered, "Kill this fag's lover, and bring him here. Then sink the boat."

"Oh, fuck no." William curled his lip as he watched the second pair of guards bound onto his deck while the first pulled his gun. "Protect yourself, lover," William ordered. "And grab the tubing rope from the storage in the hold. I'll entertain these yahoos long enough for you to cut it into lengths so you can truss 'em up."

William didn't wait for a response, trusting in his captain's cop instincts to keep him safe. With a sweep of both arms, he shifted. His arms extended and grew, splitting to become four. His legs did the same, and his torso and head grew and adjusted position, shredding his board shorts in the process.

Controlling his shift, William slammed into the shocked guards, sending them tumbling over the railing at the bow and splashing into the sea. Rolling off the deck himself, William crashed his huge body into Stiles's boat. The craft was in no way big enough to accommodate his giant squid form, and it broke apart, forcing Stiles to jump overboard.

If William could have smiled in squid form, he would have.

CHAPTER EIGHT

John stared in shock even as he grabbed the railing to steady himself. The yacht rocked dangerously as William's still-expanding form rolled off of it. Gaping, he saw how his lover in giant squid form landed directly on the other boat, causing the wood and metal to split.

Just damn!

Hearing the cries of the guards, part of John thought about helping them. Then he remembered what Stiles had ordered them to do . . . and they'd seemed okay with the orders. William was right. Something wasn't right at Perisource.

Once the rocking of the yacht evened out enough for John to safely move, he sprinted across the deck and into the cabin. His first order of business was getting to his bag. He dug out his *Glock*, which he'd rolled up in his shoulder holster and tucked in the bottom beneath his change of clothes.

John tugged on the holster, the weight familiar and comforting after being threatened by strangers. After a few seconds of thought, he remembered the hold William had spoken of. His lover had vaguely waved toward it during the short tour he'd given him when he'd first been brought aboard.

After jerking the door open, John peered inside the space. He spotted the uninflated tube as well as the rope. Even as he grabbed the coiled length, he absently wondered when they would ever use the item.

Pausing in the galley, John jerked open a drawer. He saw

the sharp knives carefully fitted into their slots. After drawing out a carving knife, he closed the drawer and returned to the deck.

John wasn't certain what he'd expected to see when he returned topside, but a giant squid—*my giant squid*—with four arms waving in the air while two more held him against the yacht, just as he'd done before wasn't it.

In each of the squid's lifted arms was a man—the three would-be assassins and their leader. One man was unconscious, his head drooping forward with his chin to his chest. Another man was bellowing obscenities. A third gaped, but if he was trying to speak, his voice box wasn't cooperating. Only the man William had called Stiles appeared to be coherent.

"Help us, you bloody fool," Stiles called, and John realized he was talking to him. "I see that gun. Shoot this abomination!"

Shaking his head, John gripped the railing. "Tell me what I want to know first. Then I'll help you," he lied. "You were going to kill me and sink William's boat. Why?" The cop in him couldn't help but interrogate the crazy bastard while he had the chance.

"Because he and his brother are trying to create problems for my boss," Stiles claimed, twisting and turning within William's grip. "No one messes with my boss, but if you help us, I'll make sure you're well compensated."

William vocalized a low, haunting sound.

John wondered if that was William's squid's way of telling Stiles off. He sure wanted to. Instead, he peered over the railing and asked his lover in animal form, "Now what?"

In response, the squid moved the arm holding the unconscious man over the deck. With a surprising amount of care, he set down the man. Then he drew his arm close to John and slid it over the coil of rope he still held.

"Ah, right." The squid's meaning couldn't have been clearer to John. "Tie them up."

John uncoiled a length of the rope and cut it off. As he crossed to the downed man, he heard Stiles shouting obscenities at him, calling him a liar and more. John ignored him.

After John had finished tying up the man's hands, he crossed to the railing and called, "Done."

William responded by swinging the open-mouthed, seemingly frozen man onto the deck. Instead of dropping him, he adjusted his coiled arm, revealing the man's hands. As John tied the guy's hands in front of him, he found himself in awe of William's control.

Since this man was awake, John trussed the guard's feet, too.

John and William repeated the process with the third guard as well as Stiles. Those men afforded a bit more of a challenge, struggling and putting up a fight. William ended up having to partially let go of them, so John could put his bad-guy take-down skills to use. That pair he tied with their hands behind their backs.

Once done, William reappeared over the railing and strode toward them. His strong, broad form gleamed with the water dripping off his skin. Comfortable with his nudity, he stopped before Stiles and scowled at him.

"Well, you and Armando are creating quite a problem for yourselves, Stiles," William stated. Then he grinned and wrapped his arm around John's waist. "You see, this is Captain John Casinov that you threatened." William snorted as he smirked at the man. "Not a good idea to threaten a cop."

Stiles sneered but wisely kept his mouth shut.

"Go put on some clothes," John grumbled, pushing him toward the cabin. William laughed, but he started moving. To distract himself from the glorious sight of his lover's flexing ass globes, John added, "I'll call my guys so they can meet us at the dock."

"Uh, no. You can't do that," William stated, pausing and half turning to look at him. "They saw me shift. We need to alter their memories first. Anonymity is damn near everything to us."

John gaped. "You can alter memories?"

William shook his head. "Not shifters. But vampires can. We have an agreement with the coven in Los Angeles," he continued, as if dropping the fact that vampires were real wasn't another earth-shattering revelation. "I'll have Kaiser contact the coven and fly someone up to take care of these guys, then you can have your people take them in."

Nodding slowly, John muttered, "Ooookay."

"John hasn't been around the last couple of days," Kaiser pointed out before lifting his iced tea to his lips and taking a drink. After swallowing, William still hadn't bothered to answer, since it wasn't really a question, so Kaiser asked, "How are you doing, Will?"

William forced a smile, then heaved a sigh. "I'm okay. He's not freaking out about me being a shifter, but that vampires are real definitely shocked the shit out of him." Rising from the chaise lounge chair, he set his own glass of iced tea into the cup slot of the plastic table. "As it turns out, processing these guys is becoming a hell of a fight. Armando has a lot of rich, sleazy lawyers. Typical."

Pushing off his board shorts, William placed them on his chaise before crossing to the yacht's railing. "John's been working a lot of long hours, but if he doesn't come over soon, I'm going to show up at his house and ambush him." Resting his ass against the railing, he told his brother, "My squid is getting impatient, and so am I. I'm also getting tired of my right hand." Turning away from Kaiser, he stated,

"I'm gonna go for a swim. Coming?"

William and Kaiser often swam together, although they didn't normally go far from their yacht.

Kaiser waved his hand and shook his head. "I'll join you shortly." He held up his tea. "I want to finish this first."

Nodding, William swung his leg over the railing and dove into the water. He shifted, letting his squid out. Diving deep, he undulated away from the yacht in search of something to nibble on.

William had been swimming underwater for only around fifteen minutes when the vibrations caused by a motor danced across his senses. Curious, he swam toward the surface. Keeping deep enough not to be noticed by anyone but the sharpest paranormal eyes, William realized it was a police boat.

The echoes of slightly distorted voices reached William, but he was still able to make out the conversation.

"Hey, there. It's Kaiser, isn't it?"

Excitement filled William upon recognizing John's voice. He barely resisted the urge to rise to the surface, but he had no idea of who else might be on the boat.

"Yes. And you must be John," Kaiser replied. "How can I help you?"

"Well, Grisham told me William was out here with you," John replied, sounding a little uncertain.

Kaiser chuckled. "He's below, deep sea diving." It was an apt analogy. "Why don't you come aboard and wait. I'm sure he won't be long."

"Thanks." John's next comment must have been to whoever was driving the police boat. "Thanks for the lift, guys. I appreciate it."

"You're welcome, Captain," someone replied. "Anytime."

Then the boat engine revved, and it started away. If

Kaiser and John shared more conversation, William couldn't hear it over the vibrations washing over his senses. Once the boat was out of earshot, William began surfacing.

"I can fetch William for you, if you wish," Kaiser was telling John. "It shouldn't take me long to find him."

William lifted an arm and tapped the deck.

"Never mind," Kaiser stated. "There he is now."

Reaching for his human form, his need to hold and kiss his human driving him, William shifted swiftly. He treaded water and peered up at the railing, spotting John staring down at him. Kaiser appeared, and for the first time in William's life, he found himself annoyed at his brother's nudity.

Except, John didn't even glance in Kaiser's direction, his attention obviously on William as he called down a greeting.

Kaiser leaped over the railing and dove into the water. A second later, he surfaced beside William. "I'll swim back." Giving William a cheeky grin, he purred, "Have fun, brother." Then Kaiser shifted, his expanding form sinking beneath the waves.

William appreciated Kaiser's thoughtfulness, then partially shifted his arm and drew himself up onto the yacht's deck. As soon as he could, he hopped over the railing and grabbed John, drawing him into his embrace. William reveled in the feel of his mate in his arms again and that he'd come to him willingly.

"Hi, handsome," William whispered roughly, clutching John to him. "I missed you."

"Missed you, too," John replied, rubbing his hands over William's shoulders. "Couldn't wait anymore, case be damned. Paperwork can wait. You can't."

Groaning, William pressed a soft kiss to John's lips. "Thank you," he whispered before sealing his mouth over John's more fully.

Thrusting his tongue between John's lips, William relished the chance to reacquaint himself with his mate's taste and feel. He teased their appendages together even as he rocked his hips. The warm give and take as John kissed him back caused his blood to heat in his veins as his arousal swelled.

William broke the kiss and rested his forehead against John's. He rubbed up and down his back, tracing the knobs of his human's spine through his shirt. "Tell me I can have you, John," William murmured huskily. "I need you. Need to complete our bond. Twine our lives for eternity."

While the vampire had been altering their attacker's memories, making them think a gas leak exploded their boat, giving John and William the chance to turn the tide and capture them, William had explained everything about the connection between them as mates and how bonding worked.

"Hell yeah," John replied, his voice just as breathy and eager. "Why do you think I talked the guys into coming out here?"

William moaned before claiming John's lips again. He kept it brief, the throbbing in his shaft too great. Then he eased his hold, took John's hand, and began leading him toward the cabin.

"Gods," William whined, gripping the base of his dick with his free hand to stay his need to come. "I gotta think about something else, or I'm gonna come."

John chuckled, knocking his shoulder into William's own. "Does it make me an asshole that I love that you need me so badly?"

"Not at all." William grinned hungrily, sweeping his focus over the jeans and t-shirt his human wore. "But don't be surprised if you occasionally lose articles of clothing due to my need."

Laughing, his hazel eyes twinkling, John nodded. "Dually

noted. Then I'll tell you now that my son called me last night."

Recalling all the harsh words that had passed between John and Jonathan, William felt his ardor cool a little. "Oh? What did he say?" he asked, stopping in the bedroom and reaching for the hem of John's t-shirt. William loved that John didn't even hesitate to lift his arms so he could remove the article.

"Surprisingly, Jonathan apologized," John told him as soon as his head appeared again. His expression appeared bemused, and he continued talking when William dropped to one knee and began taking off his man's sandals. "Evidently, Anita lost her temper and came out to him, telling him that she's a lesbian. Shocked him and forced him to come to grips with it."

William held his gaze as he began working on John's jeans. "You don't seem too surprised." His human's scent betrayed that it hadn't been much of a revelation for him.

John stepped out of his jeans, then backed away, reaching for his underwear himself. "No, Grace and I had already discussed it."

"I'm glad things are patched up with your son," William stated, rising to his feet. He narrowed his eyes as he watched John round the bed. William licked his lips as he eyed his human's gorgeous erection. "But why are you moving away from me?"

"So I could get this," John revealed, opening the nightstand and pulling out the lube.

Then John climbed onto the bed, sprawling on his back.

William's breath caught in his throat at the beautiful picture his captain made. His warm hazel eyes held a hunger that caused William's dick to leak. John's light, salt and peppered chest hair called for William's fingers to brush through it. His flat stomach led to a light thatch of curly pubic hair surrounding his thick dick, which curved upward, a bead of pre-cum already gleaming at the tip. John even had his legs spread invitingly, offering just a teasing peek of his hole.

Licking his lips, William longed for a taste of that.

John lifted his hand and beckoned to him. "Take me, William." His eyes gleamed with a surety that caused William's heart to skip a beat. "Make me yours. Bond us, mate."

Moaning, William couldn't resist an offer like that. He crawled on the bed, prowling forward. After taking the tube of lubricant from his willing human, William swallowed John's prick to the root.

William relished John's howl of pleasure and did exactly as his mate had asked, twining their lives until the end of time.

ABOUT THE AUTHOR

Charlie started writing fantasy when she was eight, and after stumbling onto her first erotic romance at age nineteen, she realized her true calling. She now focuses on writing gay erotic romance, normally of the paranormal variety, with heroes of all kinds. With the help and support of her husband, Charlie finally fulfilled one of her life-long goals . . . move to acreage with her horses. You can often find her curled up with her laptop and a cup of tea or glass of wine, creating her next adventure. Charlie enjoys exploring the mountains of her new Oregon home on horseback, 4-wheeler, or motorcycle.

She can be reached at ch.richards2010@yahoo.com

Or visit her at www.charlie-richards.com